'I'm not scared,' Pete said. 'I'll do any old test for fun. But I'm a real Fortune — no matter how it turns out.'

Just for a moment, he saw a flash of respect in Tracey's blue eyes. Just for a moment, he saw the beginning of a smile.

'We'll see about that tonight,' she said. . .

The Good Fortunes Gang is the first title in a riveting quartet of novels about a group of cousins living in a small New Zealand town. Three further titles — *A Fortunate Name*, *A Fortune Branches Out* and *Tangled Fortunes* — are also available and will be published shortly by Yearling Books.

Margaret Mahy is internationally recognized as one of today's best writers for young readers, her books having been translated into all the major languages of the world. Twice winner of the prestigious Carnegie Medal, she has also won the Esther Glen Award five times and the Observer Teenage Fiction Award once. Born in a country town in New Zealand, the oldest of a family of five, with over twenty cousins in the surrounding neighbourhood, Margaret Mahy grew up with a strong sense of being part of a close family. She lives near Christchurch in New Zealand.

To my Whakatane cousins –
in memory of happy days

THE GOOD FORTUNES GANG
A YEARLING BOOK : 0 440 86286 8

First published in Great Britain by Doubleday,
a division of Transworld Publishers Ltd

PRINTING HISTORY
Doubleday edition published 1993
Yearling edition published 1994

Set in Monotype Bembo by
Phoenix Typesetting, Ilkley, West Yorkshire

Yearling Books are published by Transworld Publishers Ltd,
61–63 Uxbridge Road, Ealing, London W5 5SA
in Australia by Transworld Publishers (Australia) Pty Ltd,
15–25 Helles Avenue, Moorebank, NSW 2170,
and in New Zealand by Transworld Publishers (NZ) Ltd,
3 William Pickering Drive, Albany, Auckland.

Reproduced, printed and bound in Great Britain by
Cox & Wyman, Reading, Berks.

MARGARET MAHY

THE GOOD FORTUNES GANG

Illustrated by John Farman

YEARLING BOOKS

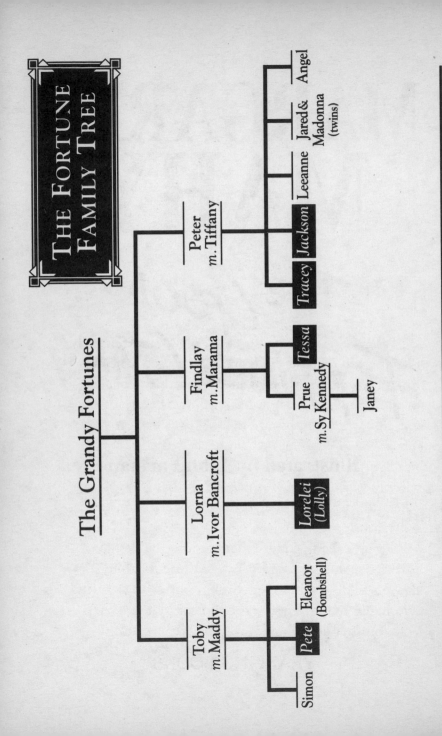

THE FORTUNE FAMILY TREE

The Grandy Fortunes

- Toby
  *m.*Maddy
  - Simon
  - Pete
  - Eleanor
    (Bombshell)
- Lorna
  *m.*Ivor Bancroft
  - Lorelei
    (Lolly)
- Findlay
  *m.*Marama
  - Prue
    m. Sy Kennedy
    - Janey
  - Tessa
- Peter
  *m.*Tiffany
  - Tracey
  - Jackson
  - Leeanne
  - Jared &
    Madonna
    (twins)
  - Angel

CHAPTER ONE

'Ice cream!' cried Pete's father, Toby, unexpectedly slowing the car as they drove into town. 'I need instant ice cream.' He glanced towards the back of the car where his sons, Simon and Peter, sat on either side of Bombshell, the baby, in her car seat. They were snugly packed in with sleeping-bags, windcheaters, pillows, and plastic bags of nappies. All the big stuff had gone on ahead of them in packing cases and was supposedly waiting for them in the new house.

'Shops!' cried Maddy, their mother, as if they had not seen shops for years. 'I'm going to buy flowers, Toby.' She opened the door of the car and scrambled out, talking as she did so. 'Then, when your mother actually sees me for the first time ever, I'll be carrying a big bunch of flowers for her. And I'll get some apples. Forget the ice cream! Ice cream's just junk food.'

'Oh, come on, Mum,' groaned Simon, impatiently flinging himself back among the sleeping-bags. He was wearing black jeans and a black T-shirt, and had spent his Christmas money having his hair dyed black. His eyebrows, however, were still fair. . . so fair that from some angles it looked as if he did not have any eyebrows at all. A thin gold earring shone in one ear. Simon looked like a teenage vampire with pimples. 'We're healthy *enough*,' he cried. 'And there's a milk bar, right there!'

'That is not a milk bar,' said his father, thrusting a red five dollar bill at Pete. 'It might be a milk bar in Australia, but we're in New Zealand now, and in New Zealand it's a dairy. Your mother can buy flowers at that shop down the road, but Pete will infiltrate the dairy and buy us ice creams. Your mother doesn't have to have one.'

'I will have one, after all,' said Maddy quickly, bending down to look through the window. 'A vanilla ice cream. Not one of those lurid ones that looks as if it's all bruised and bleeding. And no chocolate chip! Nothing speckled. They make me think huge flies have been sitting on them.'

'You certainly know how to take the fun out of an ice cream,' Toby grumbled as Pete climbed out of the car, holding the five dollar note tightly in case the wind tried to snatch it away from him. He slammed the car door behind him. He was on his own in a new world.

Pete stood for a moment, glancing left and right. Although the shops looked ordinary enough, they were still shops in another country – a land of legend – for he was standing in Fairfield, his father's home town. 'I remember, back in Fairfield . . .' his father would say, beginning a hair-raising story of his own childhood. And now the shops were Fairfield shops, those hills beyond them were the Fairfield hills, and the sky overhead was Fairfield sky. In a few minutes

he would be meeting his New Zealand grandparents
for the first time and, that afternoon, relations from
all over Fairfield would be gathering for a Fortune
family reunion. The reunion, it was agreed, had
to come before anything else. After that, Pete and
his family would be free to begin unpacking and
moving into their new house – which was also an
old house . . . the very house his father had lived in
when he was a boy.

The dairy, Pete found, turned out to be one of
those shops that sells everything you might run out
of over the weekend and can't possibly do without.
There was even a rack of videos for hire.

'*Zombie vengeance: the dead arise and take revenge
on the living,*' proclaimed the one nearest to him in
slimy green lettering.

'Four vanilla ice creams, please,' said Pete to
the woman behind the counter, and then looked
doubtfully at the five dollar note. It didn't look like
real money you could actually buy anything with.
Pete knew he would get used to it, though. A
traveller learned to get used to anything.

But then, as the woman reached for the ice cream
scoop, Pete heard a dreadful sound – half whoop,
half howl – coming from somewhere behind him.
Zombie vengeance, he thought, and spun round,
clenching his fists and gritting his teeth, prepared

to go down fighting all the way. The wild whoop became a fiendish shriek, rushing towards the shop, growing louder and louder every moment. There was a whirr of wheels and, just as the shriek dissolved into crackling, wicked laughter, two figures streamed past the shop . . . a boy and a girl, both yelling and laughing as they shot by on skateboards.

Pete saw the girl most distinctly. He stood staring, even when there was nothing more to look at, as chilly as if he had seen a ghost.

'Watch where you're going!' someone shouted angrily.

'I swear those kids'll come to grief one of these days,' said the woman behind the counter, patting generous scoops of ice cream into the cones.

But Pete was still staring at the space where the skateboarding-girl had suddenly appeared and grinned at him. He had recognized her. Although he had only been in town ten minutes, he had recognized her . . . the girl from his worst nightmare.

Pete had been having this particular nightmare for as long as he could remember, but he had never got used to it. While he was dreaming, it was always as if it were happening for the first time, and it was always terrible. As he dreamed, every single thing he was fond of – everything that made home home – crept out of his room, while other unfamiliar things crept silently in and settled down as if they had always been there. Even the windows would slide around the walls, opening in different directions on to strange new views. His parents slid, too, tiptoeing around, picking up Bombshell the baby, and waking Simon. Finally, all four of them would steal off through the front door, while two different parents, and a strange, scowling big sister, with long fair hair and sharp blue eyes, tiptoed in through the back door. In his dream, Pete would suddenly wake up and find himself surrounded by alien furniture and alien people. 'Where are Mum and Dad?' he would ask the aliens. 'Here we are, you silly boy,' the aliens would say with terrible smiles. 'We're your *real* parents and this is your sister. That other family, the ones you *think* you remember, were nothing but dreams.'

The face that had flashed in and out of sight at the shop window – the face with the fierce smile and the wild, fair hair tossing around it – had been the face of the nightmare sister. Even though his hands were by now full of ice cream, Pete felt as if the wide-awake everyday world around him had actually become frail and thin, a curtain of cobwebs which he might accidentally brush away at any moment. He was here in Fairfield, the centre of Fortune family stories. He was here, where, according to his father, they were going to stop travelling and settle down at last. But now it seemed that not only his father's family, but Pete's own worst nightmare, might be waiting for him here.

CHAPTER TWO

It was later in the day when Pete next thought about
his nightmare and the face he had glimpsed through
the shop window. He stood in an upstairs room
which was quite empty except for a bed and two
suitcases. One was still unopened, but old jeans and
a pair of underpants trailed out of the other, almost
as if they were trying to escape and rush off to join
in the Fortune family reunion without him. He was
trying to imagine this room filled with his things
– his books, his tapes, his posters – but it stayed
obstinately empty.

'Pete!' called his mother from somewhere else in
the house.

'Coming,' he replied, but he did not move.
Instead, he looked out of the window across the tops

of trees to the sea. The island on the horizon had a
feather of smoke drifting from it. It was a volcano.
Many years ago, this room had been his father's
room, and the sea and the volcano were what his
father would have seen every single morning for
years and years and years.

'Pete,' called his mother again, 'are you ready?'

'I said I was coming!' he called back.

He liked the straight, clear line where the sea met
the sky. He liked the leaves that framed the view of
the smoking island, and the rounded scoops of cloud
behind it. All the same, as he had climbed out of
the car and looked at the front of the house for the
first time, Pete had had the second shock of the day.
A second *sign*, he thought, that Fairfield was a more
dangerous place than he had ever imagined it would
be. He tried not to think about the tall hedge that
he could see from his window, or the strange, stone

faces that had smiled at him through the leaves. No wonder Simon had given such a shout of triumph and had pointed and nudged him so sharply! But Grandma Fortune had pointed towards trees on the other side of the house.

'There's a path through the trees there, to our house,' she had said. Pete was glad of an excuse to turn his back on the shadows, the hedge and the stone faces.

'Pete!' his mother called for the third time. This time he knew she really meant it.

As he left his room, he turned left. But that was a direction that belonged to the last house he had lived in. 'This is the day, but it isn't the way,' he muttered to himself. Then he thumped downstairs, singing a Fortune family song which the house must have heard many times before.

'*No matter how young a prune may be,*
It's always full of wrinkles.'

He wanted to let the house know he belonged in it.

Simon and Maddy were standing at the bottom of the stairs, face to face, like wrestlers searching for holds on one another.

'Spattzz!' muttered Simon, as Pete came downstairs. *Spattzz!* was a word Pete himself had invented so that he could swear when he needed to without being told off for it, but Simon had liked the sound of it. Already, it was more his word than Pete's.

'Spattzz and double spattzz! Just listen! He's going to be worse than ever, now we're actually going to live in Fortuneland for ever and ever.'

'We'll see,' said their mother.

'Do you mean we'll see if Pete gets worse, or we'll see if we're actually going to live here for ever and ever?'

'We'll see!' said Maddy, meaning, *Stop pestering me!*

'I know *you* don't want to live here,' said Simon. 'And Dad might change his mind in a week. I mean, he's made a few mistakes about places to live before now, hasn't he?'

'Don't you *want* to live in Fairfield?' Pete cried, staring at his mother. 'I thought you did! You said you were sick of travelling with a baby.'

'Who'd want to live a hundred miles from a proper city?' asked Simon. 'And another thing . . . why have people been moving *out* of this house? The grandparents moved out three years ago, and Uncle Peter and his family moved in. Now Uncle Peter and his family have moved out, and *we're* moving in. There's something they're not telling us, and it's more than bad drains because Uncle

Findlay's a plumber, isn't he, so if it was drains they could get them fixed cheaply.'

'Grandma and Grandpa Fortune moved out because the house was too big for them,' said Maddy.

'But it wasn't too big for Uncle Peter and his lot, though, was it?' Simon asked in a cunning voice. 'I mean, they've got six kids!'

'Uncle Peter moved out because he bought a business with a house attached to it,' their mother said, seizing Pete and looking him up and down as if she were planning to sell him and wanted him to look good.

'That's what they *say*,' said Simon. 'There's got to be more to it than that.' He gave Pete a sly, considering glance. 'I'll give you a clue. Think about what's over the hedge.'

Before he could stop them, Pete's thoughts once more made a picture of the hedge, and then sprang back from it as if it were red hot.

'No matter how young a prune may be,
It has a worried look!' he sang to himself.

Simon let out a wailing cry.

'Why does he sing *those* songs?'

'Well, why have you dyed your hair black? Why are you wearing an earring in one ear?' Maddy answered.

'That's different,' Simon said impatiently. 'That's modern . . . *trendy*. But nobody else in the world sings those double-spattzz, hairy old songs . . . nobody except Dad, and that thing there.'

'Don't call your brother "that thing there". Pete looks all right. Now . . . what about you?'

'I look cool,' said Simon.

'No matter how young a prune may be,
It's always getting stewed,' sang Pete, rolling his eyes.

Simon's own eyes narrowed. He smiled in a sinister way that made his teeth look like fangs. 'People leave this house because it's *haunted*,' he hissed, while his mother peered into his face, as if she were struggling to read something written in small print. But really she was just examining him for possible dirt.

'Let's be off!' cried Toby, bouncing through the doorway (Pete wasn't sure which room that door led to). His father was holding Bombshell, dressed up for the great Fortune family reunion his grandparents were preparing in the house on the other side of the trees.

It was all *Bombshell's* fault, Pete thought. If it hadn't been for her, Pete and his family might still be gypsies travelling around Australia, going from job to job, house to house, and school to school. But because Bombshell had forced her way into the family, here they were, standing among packing cases, preparing to meet the people belonging to all the family names found scrawled across Christmas cards, or described in stories of long ago.

'Let's go!' said Pete's mother.

Toby led the way carrying Bombshell, who waved her green bear over his shoulder. Pete and Simon fell in behind them. Simon nudged Pete. He was smiling his vampire smile again.

'Tonight you are going to have one of your ni-i-ightma-a-ares,' he hissed in a low, mysterious voice – like a wizard pronouncing a spell.

'Baby prunes look like their dad,
But not wrinkled quite as bad,' Pete sang defiantly.

'Don't forget,' said Simon, 'that from this day forward we're living next to a *graveyard*. Let's hear you sing about that!'

CHAPTER THREE

'You'll love them all,' cried Toby, jiggling Bombshell, who laughed and hit him over the head with her bear. 'And they'll love you!' he added, hugging Pete's mother with his free arm.

'It's nice to see you so happy,' she said, smiling.

'Do I *have* to go?' Simon grumbled behind them. 'I've already met the grandparents, and there's nobody else there . . . not anyone my age, I mean. All the cousins are just kids – like that thing there.'

'Except for Prue,' said his mother.

'But she's *married*,' said Simon, as if being married was a terrible, catching sickness. 'Well, she's *been* married. She's got a baby. She's old.'

'Come on, Simon, don't be shy,' said Toby.

'I'm not *shy!*' cried Simon angrily.

But suddenly Pete could see Simon *might* be shy;
that he might be hiding his shyness behind a vampire
smile. Pete didn't think he was shy himself. He was
too used to starting at new schools halfway through
the year, and to being stared at by everyone. Perhaps
it was different for Simon.

Toby was the only wanderer of the Fortune
family, yet his stories, told between packing and
unpacking, were all about being in a single place
with the same people. His stories were about his
two brothers and his only sister, about tree-houses,
and dams across creeks, and a strange game of
hide-and-seek called *worraworra*, played at night in
the family forest – Fortune's Chase – that spread up
the hill behind the house. Not only that, his songs
were funny old songs he had learned from his own
father, who had learned them from *his* father. By
now, Pete could sing them all, too . . . 'Nellie the
Nudist Queen', 'I Scream, We All Scream for Ice
Cream', and 'The Prune Song'. No matter what else
changed, the songs stayed the same – always friendly,
always jolly.

Pete's family walked across the veranda, down
the steps and on to the lawn. Ahead of them, the
hill dropped away and they could look out over
the open sea. Shadows nibbled at the golden light
washing the lawn, giving it a jigsaw-puzzle edge.

Pete turned his face towards the sunshine, but Simon nudged him and glanced meaningfully at the tall, dark hedge in the shadow behind them.

Pete laughed and looked casually back. There, staring through the leaves at the very top of the hedge, he saw, once more, those three faces — grey faces patched with moss — watching him, and smiling with closed, secret lips.

'Heh! Heh! Heh!' said Simon, giving a soft vampirish chuckle.

Somehow, Pete's father had never mentioned the old graveyard in any of his stories, let alone the tall hedge that hid most of it. Three grey angels, though, were taller still, and they peered over the top of the hedge like nosy neighbours watching someone else's family life.

Simon nudged Pete again.

'Spooky! Spooky! Spooky!' he said.

'I'm not frightened of ghosts,' Pete muttered. Yet losing a family, even in a dream, was like a sort of death. And having the same nightmare over and over again was almost like being haunted. Living next to a graveyard would only give the nightmare power.

Going through a little rickety gate, Pete and his family followed a track that wound through the bush (they called forests 'bush' in New Zealand, just as they did in Australia). Trees rose up around them, closing them in with leaves and shadows. A net of thin, twisty, unknown paths branched off and vanished under fallen leaves. In the distance they could hear happy voices . . . sounds of Fortunes, meeting and already having a good time . . . Pete, remembering his father's stories of family picnics, imagined uncles and aunts bringing bowls of salad, chocolate cakes, and all sorts of other good things into Grandma Fortune's kitchen. And they would be bringing more than sausages and cakes. They would be bringing their children too, of course.

Cousins! He was going to meet them and, in particular, four cousins of his own age – Tessa (Uncle Findlay's daughter), Tracey and Jackson (Uncle Peter's kids), and Aunt Lorna's daughter, Lolly Bancroft, the only cousin who did not have

Fortune for her last name. In a few minutes they would become more than mere names. They would be round and real. For Pete, this reunion was like the first day at a new school. In family stories, Fortunes were always true to other Fortunes. In real life he might not like his cousins. And they might not like him.

The track under the trees of Fortune's Chase was soft with leaves and fringed with ferns. Pete and his family walked over speckles of gold. The trees tangled green fingers over his head, and ferns swarmed up the banks on either side. Some ferns were as big as trees, with hairy trunks and leaves that were green above and silver below.

'On the track! No turning back!' Pete whispered to himself, talking in rhyme as he often did when he talked to himself. In spite of everything, he didn't want to turn back, but when he suddenly saw steps cut into the bank, he couldn't help stopping and staring, trying to work out where they led to. Looking into the branches above, he saw a great black patch like the nest of a dragon, nestled among the leaves of a big tree. There seemed to be some sort of climbing rope dangling from it. But as he stared upwards, Bombshell threw her bear at him, hitting him on the ear.

'Pick that up, will you?' asked his father. Pete

23

picked up the toy and followed his family once more
– out through the leaves and into a bare garden
filled with lots of people who all turned and stared
at them. Shouts of welcome sounded like one shout.
Smiles seemed like one smile.

But there were no smiles on the only face Pete
could see that was more or less on a level with his.

A thin girl with fair, straggly hair, and bright blue eyes, was actually scowling at him. Then uncles and aunts pressed forward, beaming and holding out their hands and arms, and the girl was hidden.

Pete suddenly saw himself as she must have seen him, coming out of the bush holding a green bear, just as if he were a little kid who needed a toy to comfort him. But that was not the worst thing. The worst thing was that the fair straggly hair and bright blue eyes belonged to his nightmare sister. She had been waiting for him, already more a part of the family than he was.

CHAPTER FOUR

Suddenly, there were Fortunes all around him,
telling him their names. So this was Uncle Findlay,
fair and freckled, and this was Aunt Marama,
with black hair piled on top of her head, and dark
Polynesian skin. 'Pete, here's Uncle Peter, the one
you were named after,' said his mother. 'And this is
Aunt Tiffany.' Pete knew it would take him a long
time to remember which face belonged to which
aunt or uncle. He just smiled, and let the uncles
shake his hand and pat his back, and the aunts kiss
him. They didn't really want him to say much, just
to smile and show he was happy to be among them.
As for cousins, there were cousins everywhere.

   The tallest and oldest was Prue, Uncle Findlay's
daughter, carrying in her arms a baby older than

Bombshell. She and the baby, Janey, were still living
with Uncle Findlay and Aunt Marama, although
she was nineteen and had once been married. For
the family reunion, Prue had chosen to wear an
old, white floating dress of material which had
been painted with golden suns and silver moons.
She also wore black lace tights, and sneakers, dyed
green. Pete noticed Simon's mouth fall open for a
moment when he first saw Prue. Then he saw him
grin, thrilled to have a cousin who looked almost as
trendy as he thought he did himself.

Meanwhile, Leeanne, the middle daughter of Uncle Peter and Aunt Tiffany, stared at Simon and then began to follow him. She was about eight years old, and carried a Barbie doll. Simon pretended not to see her.

Most of the other cousins were small. Several of them were babies whose names Pete could not remember, Uncle Peter's three-year-old twins among them. People smiled at the babies trying to make them smile back, telling one another over and over again that the babies were 'real Fortunes'. If they stayed here . . . if they *did* stay . . . Bombshell would grow up with cousins of her own age all around her.

'Peter, this is Lorelei,' said yet another aunt . . . his father's sister, Lorna Bancroft. Pete turned, half expecting to see the scowling girl. But this was an entirely different cousin. Lorelei Bancroft was smiling a timid, apologetic smile. Though she was ten, almost as old as Pete, she looked so shy that Pete immediately felt shy, too. When she smiled, she covered her mouth with her hand so that people couldn't see her wired-up teeth. They looked at each other in silence.

'Everyone calls me Pete, not Peter,' Pete said at last, and Lorelei suddenly looked much less shy.

'Everyone calls me Lolly,' she replied. 'Even my

mother does, when she's not thinking. Did you get that Christmas card I sent you?' Pete suddenly remembered Lolly's Christmas card. It had had a picture of Santa Claus filling the Christmas stocking of a dinosaur, and she had drawn it herself.

'It was great,' he said politely.

'The dinosaur was a diplodocus,' said Lolly. 'They'd have had enormous stockings! Are you glad to be here?'

'It's OK,' said Pete. 'OK so far!'

'Lolly,' said a voice. It was her father, Pete's Uncle Ivor. 'Your mother says she's left the keys in the car. Would you run down and get them for me?'

Lolly set off. She did not invite Pete to go with her, and, left on his own again, he moved through the crowd, grinning and nodding. Where were the other cousins who were his age? Were they actually hiding from him? He wondered how it was that he could feel that he didn't want to meet them, and yet at the same time that he had been wanting to meet them since he was a baby.

'How do you think *you'll* like living here, though?' asked a voice somewhere over his head. It was Prue talking to his mother.

'Well, it's fine so far,' said his mother, 'and this is a great party.'

To Pete's surprise, Prue laughed.

'You don't have to be polite about it – not to me,' she said. 'Did you really *want* to settle down here? After living in Brisbane and Rockhampton and Mackay, and all those other places?'

Maddy laughed, too. When she spoke her voice sounded happier for some reason.

'I don't know,' she said. 'We certainly mean to try, but by now it's hard to imagine really settling down, in spite of all the talk. Toby's always been restless. And Fairfield is a small town.'

Big enough to hold the Fortune family, thought Pete. Big enough to hold his father's stories of family *worraworras*. He remembered his old blue jeans and underpants trying to escape from his suitcase. Suppose they simply wanted to get out of the suitcase and settle down? But in his imagination the suitcase sucked them back into itself, tidied itself up, closed its own lid, and locked itself. It was like a film running backwards. Pete suddenly realized that, after such a lengthy journey and all the stories, he wanted to stay in Fairfield for a long, long time. But was there any point in trying to find cousins who didn't want to be found? Was there any point in making them notice you, when your father might get restless, in spite of all his promises?

A few steps further on, he came across his father talking to Uncle Peter. Pete listened. To his surprise

they were talking as stiffly and politely as he and
Lolly had been talking a moment earlier. They did
not sound like brothers who had built dams together
and played *worraworra* in the bush at night. If one of
them made a joke, the other one sounded unsure
about just when to laugh.

'How do you think you'll enjoy being back here?'
Uncle Peter was saying. Everyone was asking the
same question.

'Well, it is *home*,' Toby said, sounding slightly
indignant.

'Home? What do you mean by home, these days?
Let's face it, Toby, you've been away for years,'
Uncle Peter replied. 'You must have changed.'

'Hi,' said a voice so close to Pete's ear that
he knew before he turned that someone his size
was speaking to him. 'Me again!' While Pete had
been working his way in a rough circle around his
grandparents' garden, Lolly had found the car keys
and given them to her father. By now, Pete had a
question that needed an answer. 'Aren't the other
cousins here?' he asked.

'Yes, but they sneaked off,' said Lolly. 'I saw them
going into the bush. They're probably having a gang
meeting.'

'A gang?' It sounded like good fun. 'Why didn't
you sneak off too?' Pete asked.

'They call it the Good Fortunes Gang, and my name's Bancroft, not Fortune,' Lolly said. 'Only people called Fortune can belong to it.'

This seemed unfair to Pete. It wasn't Lolly's fault that Aunt Lorna had had to change her name to Bancroft when she married. He looked at Lolly, trying hard to work out if she felt sad at not belonging to the Good Fortunes Gang.

'What do they do?' he asked.

She shrugged. 'I don't know,' she said. 'I only hear them talking about it. Tessa wants to call it the Fortune Investment Society and make money. But Tracey and Jackson want it to be a gang of radical revolutionaries hiding in the forest.'

'*My* name's Fortune,' said Pete. 'I could belong.'

And suddenly he made up his mind that he would find the gang and show them that *he* was a Fortune and that they could not keep him out simply by scowling and hiding. The steps! he thought. The steps cut into the bank! The dragon's nest up in the tree!

'Shall we track them?' he asked. 'Shall we find them and make them let us join the club?'

'It's hard to make Tracey do anything if she doesn't want to,' said Lolly doubtfully. All the same, she seemed to be considering his idea. But at that moment her father called her again, and once more Pete was left on his own.

He looked around. Uncles and aunts were everywhere, talking or fussing over little kids. Simon was talking to Prue. His parents had their backs to him. No-one noticed him setting out all alone into the forest, searching for people he had never met before, who obviously did not want to meet him.

CHAPTER FIVE

These trees were all Fortune trees, the path that
led between them was a Fortune path. Pete was
a Fortune, and he had come home. All the same,
this forest he was walking through did not feel
like his forest – not yet. It was watching him, not
welcoming him.

Pete walked on between trees and ferns that
would always be green, for this was a land where
the only trees that lost their leaves in autumn came
from other countries. He imagined himself as a tree
growing among these Fortune trees, as green and
leafy as any other tree. Suddenly, winter would
come. All his leaves would drop off, leaving him
naked to the icy wind. Everyone would see at a
glance that he didn't belong in that particular forest.

Behind him he could hear the babble of the family reunion, but as he rounded a bend he suddenly heard new voices. They were faint but clear, and seemed to be coming out of the air. Pete moved softly, careful not to snap twigs or rustle ferns. The voices were talking about money.

'We've got five dollars and sixty-three cents,' one voice was saying. 'My vote is that we save it up and buy shares with it. You know – invest it! We could be rich by the time we're twenty.'

'Twenty! No way! Too long, man! I won't *live* to be *twenty*,' said a second voice, sounding very cheerful.

'Well, *I* vote we slide down to the road by one of the tracks and invest the money in fish and chips right now,' said a third voice. 'I'm not going back to be reunioned with Australians.'

'They're half New Zealanders,' said the first voice.

The voices, Pete realized, were up in the dragon's nest . . . the biggest nest in the world. No. Not a nest. A platform! Pete had found a Fortune family tree-house, and the Good Fortunes Gang were having a meeting. What now? Should he shake the tree and force his cousins to notice him? He imagined shaking it with super-strength so that cousins came tumbling down like ripe apples.

'It's not a crime, and now's the time,' he

muttered, and began pulling his way up steps in the bank, grabbing handfuls of ferns, and then a knobbly root to steady himself.

'I've really *had* it with family reunions. Who cares!' said the third voice. 'I'm not going to be friendly with kids who pushed us out of our house.'

'Your dad bought the car yard,' the first voice said. 'You'd have moved, anyway.'

Pete knew at once that the knobbly root was used to being held. Other hands had polished it. The narrow steps fitted his size of foot exactly. A tug, a heave, and he was safely up, one hand on the tree trunk. A rope with knots in it, a climbing rope, dangled from the branch, and there were slats of wood nailed to the side of the tree, making a rough ladder. Pete thought the rope would be the most daring way to climb. He kicked off his sandals, seized the rope, and swarmed upwards.

The people on the platform in the tree suddenly fell silent. They could feel him struggling as he clambered, hand over hand, clamping his feet around

each knot, pushing upwards, swinging like a monkey
king. No-one looked out to help or hinder him.
Nailed to the edge of the platform was a painted
sign. *The Good Fortunes Gang*, it said in faded,
uneven lettering. As Pete read it, the rope swung
towards the notice until the words seemed as big as
the world. They were all he could see. A moment
later his nose was mashed against them. Pete refused
to groan. Instead, he hooked the fingers first of one
hand and then the other around the edge of the
platform and hung there, breathing, and letting his

nose recover. Then he pulled himself up so that he was propped on his forearms, looking over the edge of the platform.

Three faces stared back at him. That must be Tessa, the younger sister of Prue, with black curls and skin that was darker than her father's but paler than her mother's. That must be Jackson, the boy whose blond hair was clipped short and stubbly on top, leaving long, pale locks hanging down around his neck. Even though he was up a tree and in the shade, Jackson had his nose covered with blue zinc ointment. He looked like a surfer.

The third face was the one he already knew. That was scowling Tracey, her hair as fair as Jackson's. Pete noticed how the other two looked at her as if she were their leader and they must follow her commands.

'Hi!' said Tessa at last, grinning widely. 'Did Lolly tell you where we were?'

'Are you Pete?' asked Jackson. Then, without waiting for an answer, he asked, 'What's it like in Australia?' He seemed to want to be friendly. But Pete saw Tracey push her knuckles firmly into his shoulder. Jackson fell silent, and the Good Fortunes Gang watched as Pete scrabbled and scrambled, uninvited, to swing a knee up on to the platform. None of them offered to help him.

CHAPTER SIX

Now he was on the tree-house platform, Pete felt he *must* make himself into a real Fortune. He must stop being a stranger swinging on a rope on the edge of things. But Pete could tell that Tracey was the one who did the inviting for all three cousins. And now, as he looked at her, he suddenly remembered a family photograph Uncle Peter and Aunt Tiffany had sent them years ago. Even as a little girl she had looked at the photographer with the same unsmiling and slightly menacing expression. That expression had somehow worked its way into his dreams and had settled on the face of the false sister in his nightmare.

Jackson glanced sideways at Tracey, and then copied her suspicious expression as well as he could, though it didn't quite fit his kind of face.

'What are you doing here, man?' he asked, trying to make his croaky voice sound rough and stern. 'This is *our* house.'

'It says Good Fortunes,' said Pete, pulling himself up and sitting on the edge of the platform. 'And I'm a Fortune.'

'Yes, but are you *good*?' Tessa asked, and he saw the beginning of a grin that would be wide and curly if she grinned properly.

'Pretty good,' Pete said, grinning back.

Tracey spoke. She and Jackson both had croaky voices, but it was not because they had colds. It was just the way their voices always sounded.

'Tracey,' she said, introducing herself, though Pete knew perfectly well who she must be. 'Trace the Ace!' she added now, staring hard at Pete with those bright blue eyes. Pete knew she was eleven, a little older than he was. 'Have you moved in yet?' she enquired, as if she were asking a disagreeable question.

'We haven't unpacked,' said Pete.

'Which room do *you* have?' she asked.

'It's upstairs,' Pete said. 'It's only a little one.'

'Can you see the sea from the window?' she asked, looking as thunderous as possible for someone who was so very fair. Pete nodded. 'That used to be *my* room,' she cried, screwing up her eyes angrily.

'My dad says it used to be his,' Pete said quickly.
Tracey opened her eyes in astonishment.

'But that was ages ago,' she said at last. 'That was
in history. I'm talking about modern times.'

Pete shrugged.

'It's not my fault,' he said. 'I just go where I'm
put.'

'Anyhow, what are you doing up here?' asked
Jackson.

'Perhaps he wants to join our club?' suggested
Tessa, looking slyly at Tracey. 'First, his name's
Fortune, and, second, he could *pay* to join. We need
a new financial member.' She looked over at Pete,
and then rattled a tin at him.

'Hey, listen . . . he can't just waltz in here taking
over other people's bedrooms and calling himself a
Fortune,' Tracey said, looking indignantly from one
to the other.

'No way, man!' said Jackson, watching Tracey and copying her.

'I didn't call myself a Fortune,' Pete argued, doing his best to stick up for himself, and yet trying to sound friendly at the same time. 'I was born one.'

'But you haven't lived here the way we have!' cried Tracey. Her white-blonde hair seemed to shine in the dark. She did not look quite like a girl, but she did not look like a boy, either. She looked like a burning creature from another world. 'You've taken over the old house, *my* house, and everyone's making a fuss because your lot have come home at last. But that doesn't make you a real New Zealand Fortune – like we are.'

The other two watched her respectfully. Pete hesitated, and Tracey saw him hesitate.

'Being a Fortune isn't just being *called* Fortune,' she declared. 'You get to be a true Fortune by going through the TEST. The TEST changes your blood.'

She said the word 'test' as if it were underlined. Somewhere in Pete's mind the word wrote itself in heavy black letters and then sprouted scrolls of red and gold. Jackson and Tessa looked sharply at Tracey. Pete could see they did not have any idea of what she was talking about. She had invented the idea of the test only a minute before. All the same, Jackson leaped to his feet and began dancing on the

THE GOOD FORTUNES GANG

spot, clapping his hands over his head and swaying from side to side. The platform trembled as he danced.

'Hey, man . . . the test, the test, the test!' Jackson cried. 'You've got to do the test, man, and show you are the best, man, and then we'll be impressed, man! Yay, yay, yay,' he sang. (Did rhymes run in the blood of the Fortune family? Pete wondered.)

Tracey thumped Jackson. Pete winced in sympathy. Jackson stopped dancing and fell silent, rubbing his leg where the thump had landed.

'I am secretary of this society,' Tessa said in an important voice. She smiled to herself. 'This must be recorded in the minutes,' she went on, scribbling on a pad. 'Will those in favour please say "Aye"?'

'Yeah!' said Tracey.

Tessa turned to Tracey with an indignant look.

'You've got to say *Aye*,' she insisted. 'That makes it proper, legal society business. You don't just say "yeah" – not for legal society business.'

'OK! OK! Aye, then! Aye!' groaned Tracey.

'Ai, Ai, Ai!' cried Jackson, dancing again and pretending to play a guitar. Then he made a peculiar rattling sound like drummers warming everyone up for 'God Save the Queen'.

'Jackson's musical,' said Tessa, staring at Jackson proudly. 'Are you musical?' she asked Pete.

'Everyone says I can't sing,' said Pete, watching as Tracey wrapped one thin arm around Jackson's legs and yanked his feet from under him. When he crumpled down on top of her, she seized his ears and, using them as handles, wobbled his head from side to side. He didn't seem to mind.

'Say "Aye" properly,' she cried. 'I had to.'

'Aye!' cried Jackson, his voice more froggy than ever.

Tracey looked back at Pete.

'Can't you sing?' she asked him.

Pete actually thought he sang well, but no-one in his family agreed with him. He thought he had better say no. Tracey looked pleased.

'But my dad plays the banjo,' he added, to show there was music in the family. Tracey's blue eyes had seemed almost friendly. Now, they grew sinister.

'Actually, we can have the test straightaway,' she said. 'It's a word test. If you know the right words . . . well, that proves you're a good Fortune.'

Pete's heart sank. How could he possibly know secret words when he'd only been in the country for one day.

Tracey nudged Jackson. 'OK! Sing a bit of that song and let him finish it,' she commanded.

'What song?' asked Jackson.

Tracey nudged him again. 'You know! That *prune* song!' she said.

CHAPTER SEVEN

Jackson slowly stood up.

'This is a mystical Fortune song,' Tracey announced. 'Every Fortune who is a true Fortune knows the words of this song. Go on, Jackson.'

Jackson looked as if he weren't too sure of the words himself. All the same, after a moment he began to sing.

'*No matter how old a prune may be,*
It's always full of wrinkles . . .'

'Stop!' shouted Tracey. She looked at Pete challengingly.

'Finish that song!' she ordered. 'Every true Fortune can finish that song.'

Pete had known the song for so many years that the words were part of his memory. But just for the moment he couldn't think of one of them.

'Shall I sing it again?' Jackson asked.

'No! Once is enough,' Tracey replied quickly.

But suddenly Pete remembered standing at the bottom of the stairs only half an hour ago, teasing Simon. Every single word of the song rushed back into his head, all jostling and anxious to be sung.

'It's "young"!' he said. 'Not "old". *No matter how* young *a prune may be . . .*' He began to sing.

'It's always full of wrinkles.

We may get them on our face.

Prunes get them every place.'

He sang the first verse and chorus, then the second verse and chorus. The three cousins listened intently until Pete had finished the song.

'He got it right,' said Tessa, sounding surprised.

'Yes, but that's just one song,' said Tracey quickly. 'Anyone can accidentally know *one* song. Jackson . . . do another.'

'I scream, you scream, we all scream for ice cream,' Jackson sang obediently. But after the first few words Pete joined in and sang, too. When it came to the second verse Jackson hesitated, pretending he was getting tired of singing, but Pete could easily see he had forgotten the words. Jackson might be able to sing in tune but he didn't know things by heart, the way Pete did.

'What about "Shut the Door, They're Coming

47

Through the Window"?' suggested Tessa. She began to sing herself. Jackson and Pete joined in.

'Shut the door, they're coming through the
  window.
Shut the window, they're coming through the
  door.
Shut the door, they're coming through the
  window.
Oh, the place is full, and won't hold any more!'

Tracey did not sing along. Pete had said he couldn't sing, and she had been tricked into thinking that someone who couldn't sing wouldn't know the words. As Pete, Jackson and Tessa sang the first verse and the chorus, and then the second verse and the chorus, Tracey looked more and more like the false sister of Pete's nightmare. Both Jackson and Tessa stopped singing at the end of the second chorus. They seemed to think the song was over. Pete hesitated.

'What about the third verse?' he asked.

'There isn't a third verse,' said Tracey.

'Yes, there is,' Pete cried. 'I thought every single Fortune would know the third verse. If you don't know the *third* verse you can't be a real Fortune.

Tracey looked sharply at Jackson. 'Is there a third verse?' she asked.

Jackson shrugged so hard that his shoulders came right up to his ears.

'There is, and I know it, so that means I must be *more* of a Fortune than you because I know the songs better,' cried Pete triumphantly.

Tracey's blue eyes seemed to drill through Pete.

'You can't possibly ever in this world be more of a Fortune than we are!' she cried.

'You said words were the test, and I know more words than you kids,' Pete pointed out.

'Words are only *part* of the test,' cried Tracey.

'Hey, Trace! Come off it,' said Tessa. 'Be fair!'

'Words are only the *first* part of the test,' Tracey persisted. Anyone could tell she was thinking quickly, inventing a new test as she went along. 'It's like taking a driver's test . . . you answer questions and then you do the *practical* part . . . the actual driving. He's still got to do the *practical* part.'

'Shall I do it now?' asked Pete, feeling full of confidence.

'Listen,' said Tracey, 'this reunion's probably going on for hours and hours. We've got sleeping-bags and we'll be sleeping over at the old place (*our* old place that is. It's a new place to *you*) while the grown-ups have a bit of a rave-up. That's when we'll tell you what the *practical* test is. If you get through it, we'll count you as a real Fortune.'

'Not fair!' began Tessa doubtfully. 'We should vote. That's democratic.'

'Jackson agrees with me,' said Tracey. 'That's democratic enough.' Jackson wiggled his eyebrows up and down, and swayed a little.

'Ai, ai, ai!' he sang softly.

'I'm not scared,' Pete said. 'I'll do any old test for fun. But I'm a real Fortune – no matter how it turns out.'

Just for a moment, he saw a flash of respect in Tracey's blue eyes. Just for a moment, he saw the beginning of a smile.

'We'll see about that tonight,' she said, looking tough once more. 'All right, then! Let's go back to the great reunion barbecue. I'm hungry.'

'The meeting of the Good Fortunes Gang is now adjourned,' said Tessa, sounding grown-up and important. 'Now, we'll go to the grandys' for the barbecue and make out we're ordinary.' She looked at Pete. 'That's what we do,' she said. 'Pretend to be ordinary. But secretly we're radical, especially Jackson. He's radical *and* musical, too.'

'If anyone says anything bad about a Fortune, we get our gang on to them,' Jackson said. 'That's a gang rule. We even stick up for Lolly, though she's only a Bancroft and goes to the Catholic school. Come on . . . let's go!'

CHAPTER EIGHT

Later that evening, well after the babies, the twins and Leeanne had been put to bed, Pete's mother, together with Aunt Lorna and Aunt Marama, led the big children along the track through Fortune's Chase to the old house.

Tracey nudged Pete.

'All *right*!' he hissed, before she could say anything. 'I won't forget.'

'It really *is* our house,' said Tracey, 'even if we don't live in it any more. And now we're having to sleep out in the *whare*.'

The *whare* was a little cabin with six bunks in the yard behind the old house. Pete hadn't even known it was there until the others told him about it. *Whare*, Tessa explained, was a Maori word, meaning a home.

'And no tricks either,' Pete heard Aunt Marama saying in a typically cynical mother's voice. Tricks? There were certainly going to be a few tricks after the grown-ups had gone back to the family reunion.

Lolly Bancroft was not allowed to sleep out in the *whare* . . . or perhaps she was too shy to ask. Her mother swept her into the big house, saying rather apologetically that she was frightened of bush rats, but a little earlier Pete had heard Uncle Ivor complaining to Aunt Lorna that the *whare* was filled with rubbish. Separated from the other cousins, Lolly was tucked down in a spare bedroom at the foot of the stairs.

'Wait five minutes after your mother's gone and then come down and meet us in the yard,' Tracey had said. 'Say, ten minutes, because sometimes our lot of wrinklies try to be clever and sneak back to check on Jackson and me.'

'My mother trusts me,' Tessa had smugly replied.

'What an idiot!' Tracey had muttered rudely.

In a way Pete had enjoyed sitting on the sunny edge of his grandparents' lawn, eating sausages with his cousins while planning to sneak out at night. The idea of the test brought them together, though they were the testers and he was the one being tested. He tried not to think too much about what the test might be.

As he changed into his pyjamas, Pete heard his
mother talking to Lorna and Marama at the foot of
the stairs. Then he heard Maddy climbing towards
him. He dived into bed and tried to look sleepy.

'Well,' she said, sitting on the edge of the bed.
'How has it been so far?'

'OK!' said Pete, pretending to yawn. Then he
glanced over at her and found she was staring at him
with a suspicious, motherly expression.

'OK?' she said, and pretended to yawn, too. 'As
good as that? Have the cousins been giving you a
hard time?'

'No!' he exclaimed. 'I'm not scared of them.'

'Marama tells me that Tracey is a bit of a hard
case.'

'She's all right,' said Pete. 'I'm a hard case, too.'

His mother laughed and looked happier.

'I know you are,' she said, and then gave him a kiss on his ear.

'Why do we have to go to bed now?' Pete asked.

'Because . . !'

'Why because? Everyone else is having a good time.'

'Because it's late, and, party or no party, we've got a busy day tomorrow. Unpacking! Mind you, I don't think your father will feel like getting up early.'

She turned to go, pausing at the doorway to switch out the light.

'Mum . . .' Pete called softly after her.

'Yes?'

He could not see her face, just her black shape in the doorway.

'Mum, have the aunts been giving *you* a hard time?'

'No,' she said. 'If anything, just the opposite. They've been a bit too nice to me. It makes me feel like a visitor.'

'Mum, don't you want to live here for ever?'

'Nothing lives anywhere for ever,' she answered.

'No, but you know what I mean.'

Pete was quite prepared for her to say, 'We'll see!' but she didn't. Instead, she seemed to think about it

. . . a faceless black shape leaning on the doorway.

'Well, do *you*?' she said at last.

Pete had to think about this.

'I sort of do,' he said at last. 'I want to have a place that stays still.'

'Places stay still. We're the ones that keep moving,' she replied. 'And if we don't move one way, we move another.'

'Tracey and Jackson say we took their house,' he said.

'Well, we didn't,' his mother replied. 'Uncle Peter just decided to move out months before we decided to move in. Uncle Peter gave up the crane-hire business, and your father's taken it on. We'll give it a go, shall we? I know it's all strange, but we're used to that. So let's be patient and see what happens.'

'I won't enjoy it if you don't,' he said.

His mother sighed.

'Well, my family isn't as big as your father's,' she said at last, 'and I don't think I'll miss them in the way your father missed his family. Oh, he wanted to get away from home all right, but once he was away from it, nowhere else ever felt like the right place to him. But as for me . . . I don't know how happy I'm going to be staying here. How can I tell until I've tried?'

'Will I have to cheer for the New Zealand cricket team now?' asked Pete.

'No way,' said his mother. 'You cheer for whoever you want to, mate. Now, go to sleep. And if you dream, wake up and turn the torch on. It's right beside your bed.'

'I'm not scared of dreams . . . well, just that *worst* dream,' said Pete. 'The dream of the false family.'

'Well, I've noticed that whenever we move that dream comes back,' said his mother. 'Just laugh at the false family. *We're* the real one.'

'In the dream they say they're real, and it *seems* real,' Pete groaned.

'Laugh at them,' she repeated. 'Shine the light on them.'

'Mum,' said Pete. 'Tracey looks like the girl in my dream.'

'Really?' said his mother. She sounded interested. 'It'll be because of that photograph of her. Remember, we used to have all those family photographs pinned to the wall when we were living in Mackay. There was a photograph of Tracey. She was only little then, of course, but she still looked a really hard case. I think she was probably even a hard-case baby. If you'd like me to stay close for a while, I will.'

Pete was tempted. He could imagine himself

saying, 'I would have joined you and gone through the test, no trouble at all, only my mother was feeling lonely. I had to keep her company.' But the cousins would probably guess the truth. And besides, he wanted them to admit what he himself already knew: that he was just as much a Fortune as they were.

'I'm fine,' he said. He pulled the blankets around his ears. His mother smiled, turned out the light, and went downstairs.

CHAPTER NINE

When it felt as if his mother must be safely back with the other grown-ups, Pete got up again, put on his dressing-gown, seized the torch, and went boldly downstairs. The light of his torch picked out packing cases and boxes. This isn't *anyone's* home, thought Pete. Not any more. Not yet! But if he passed the test he would win a home as his reward. He went out into the backyard.

It was a moony night. Could that possibly be the same moon Pete had seen in Australia a day or two earlier, a bright, thin sideways smile in the early evening? Now, it was rounder and whiter and seen from a different country. Pete looked up at it, imagining it was an opening of some kind, and that aliens, hidden on the other side of the sky, were sucking colours out of the world. 'Mmmm! *Red!*' he imagined them saying. 'Blue . . . delicious!'

Pete shone the torch around. The backyard certainly looked colourless as well as completely empty. He hoped his cousins had all gone to sleep. Then he would be able to go back to bed. 'Some test!' he would say in the morning, smiling scornfully. 'Walking all the way downstairs and then back up again. Really hard! Really scary.' But then a shadow on the edge of the other shadows waved at him. He sighed and made his way across the yard.

'You won't need a torch,' Tracey said, as Pete came up to them.

'You know your way round and I don't,' he answered quickly, switching the torch on and swinging the beam of light around the yard. Tracey was holding a pillow. Behind her, Jackson seemed to be carrying the skin of a giant caterpillar over his shoulder.

'Let him have it,' said Tessa. 'Let's record the beginning of the test.' She lifted her arm and stared at her own wrist just as if she were checking some delicate instrument strapped there. 'Test begun at twenty-one hours.' However, she could not possibly have read her watch in the silver-grey light of the moon.

'Tessa's got a watch that still goes when you're a thousand fathoms under the sea,' Tracey told Pete. 'It tells you the time in Tokyo, and it tells you whether it's going to be a new moon or not.' She was leading the way out of the yard and around the side of the house. She didn't need a torch. It was as if she remembered paths in the way Pete remembered the words of songs.

But then, suddenly, Pete knew exactly where they were taking him. The night was warm, but he turned cold with horror. Every part of him longed to scramble back into bed and sink into immediate sleep. He did not want to be out in the night following Tessa, Tracey and Jackson towards the graveyard.

The high, uneven hedge of laurels blocked their way. Pete could not see either angels or ghosts, but he could feel their blank eyes peering around for him. Suddenly he felt that those angels had always been there in his nightmare, staring in at the sliding windows of the changing house, smiling at his confusion and horror.

'Through here,' whispered Tracey. 'Lucky we're not fat!' Leading the way, she slipped between the twiggy branches.

'We made a door,' hissed Jackson. 'A door-a-door-a-door-a-door!' he chanted softly, drumming the air.

'Shut up!' Tracey snapped. 'Stop drumming! You want to wake the dead?' Jackson fell silent.

'Come *on*!' hissed Tracey. Tessa followed obediently. Pete came next, twisting sideways to get through the narrow gap. Jackson was last of all. The caterpillar skin caught on twigs as he came. It was a sleeping-bag.

'No-one could hear me drumming,' Jackson said to Tracey.

'The dead might,' she said. Her matter-of-fact voice was more scary than a ghostly one. 'They hear all! Right now, they can hear us entering their kingdom. That's scientifically proven.'

They were in the graveyard. There was an old grave beside them with a little wooden picket fence around it. Some of the pickets had broken away.

The grave grinned a pointed grin, with a few teeth missing. Pete looked past it. Moonlight gleamed on the edges of stone after stone, stepping down the hillside in an irregular stair.

Off they went between the graves. There were flat, sealed graves with neat headstones, and untidy, sprawling ones where flowers and weeds had taken over. Some graves were small, narrow and plain. Some were covered with slabs as big as tables. Chipped urns, fingers of marble, and grey angels with bowed heads, rose up every now and then. Pete noticed one angel that had had both wings broken off. He felt sorry for it – it could never fly again.

Then Tracey stopped so suddenly that they all bumped into one another.

'This is a good place,' she said.

'What for?' asked Pete, trying to sound slightly bored.

'For sleeping! That's the test. You have to sleep all night in the graveyard.'

Pete suddenly switched on the torch and shone it on her face. Just as he had suspected: she was smiling slyly. 'Look down there, not at me!' she cried. 'There's grass between those two stones. It'll be comfortable there. And I've brought a pillow, and Jackson's brought a sleeping-bag for you.'

'Mine!' said Jackson. 'It's my sleeping-bag, man!'

'You can keep it,' Pete said. 'It's not cold.' He was surprised at how calm his voice sounded.

'No, go on!' said Tracey. 'It gets really cold here after midnight, even on the hottest night. Cold and clammy.'

Pete took the sleeping-bag as if he didn't care one way or the other. I could stay here for an hour or two and then sneak home and get back into bed, he thought to himself. Jackson saw him smiling as he wriggled the sleeping-bag up around his shoulders.

'He might sneak back again,' said Jackson.

'Jackson's a thought-reader,' Tracey said. 'Musical people can read thoughts. OK, Pete! You've got to swear an oath. That's part of the test. Say "I, Peter Fortune . . ."'

'I, Peter Fortune . . .' said Pete wearily.

'Promise . . .'

'Promise . . .' said Pete, secretly crossing his fingers so that it would not be a real promise.

'. . . not to go sneaking back to the house, and if I even *think* of sneaking back, may bony hands come out from the ground and grab my ankles and drag me down for ever.'

Pete echoed Tracey, crossing his fingers even more tightly. Everyone in the world, he reckoned, was frightened of bony fingers grabbing them and pulling them down.

Tessa said nothing. Pete thought she looked a little worried, a little ashamed of what the Good Fortunes Gang were doing to another Fortune cousin, but Tracey was the one who was making the rules.

'OK,' Tracey said. 'This is the practical test. All you have to do is spend the night here. That's all. You only have to do it once.'

'Have you done it?' asked Pete.

'We live here. We've spent hours and hours in the burying ground,' Tracey said haughtily.

But suddenly Pete was sure that, though Tracey and Jackson might have spent hours in the graveyard, neither of them had ever slept a night there. If he did it, it would be like knowing more words to the Fortune family songs than they did. It would prove that he was not only braver than they were, but more of a Fortune, too. And they would have to admit it.

Tracey tugged at Jackson's arm.

'We're going to be watching you,' she said to Pete. 'No sneaking back!'

'I won't sneak back,' snapped Pete.

Tessa turned. She still hadn't said a single word. Tracey and Jackson turned, too. Off they went down the path between the stones, Jackson with a skip in his step as if plain walking just wasn't good enough for him. Dark Tessa disappeared into the shadows almost at once, but the fair hair of Tracey and Jackson shone in the faint moonlight. From a distance they looked like graveyard angels come down from their plinths, walking around in the dark. As the path dipped downhill, it seemed as if they were slowly sinking into the ground.

Pete sank down in turn, down on to the grass between the two headstones, hobbled by the sleeping-bag. If something did come for me, I couldn't run, he thought. He put the pillow under his head and lay on his back – waiting for morning and staring at the moon, alone in the graveyard between two tall stones.

CHAPTER TEN

'In the graveyard,' murmured Pete to himself.

   'Lying in the graveyard on my own, own, own,
   Listening for the rattle of a bone, bone, bone.'
He drew his elbows into the sleeping-bag, next to
his warm, living sides, so they would not touch the
cold, still stone.

'Now!' he said aloud, as if he were going to
arrange things efficiently. Moving his arms carefully,
he switched on the torch. The first thing he saw was
a pair of grey feet. Above the feet were the straight,
grey folds of a long robe. A chipped, grey face stared
down on him. It was another stone angel with short
curls, and a broken nose which made it look like a
boxer. The wind blew. Did the curls move? No . . .
it was simply his own trembling hand, shaking the
torch slightly so that the light trembled, too.

Pete shut his eyes and tried to trick himself into thinking he was really in bed. Of course, even if he were asleep in bed, he might be dreaming. His nightmare about the false family was a dream of losing everything which kept him safe – everything he loved. It was a dream of a sort of dying. But lying between the graves, he found, to his surprise, the nightmare had made him tough in some way. It was as if he had been practising for this test, even though he didn't know he would ever be tested.

'I'm not scared, not really,' he told himself. But why, then, did he have his eyes shut?

Pete opened his eyes. He looked straight up into the sky through thousands of miles, millions upon millions of miles, of space. All that sky, all that night that seemed to be pressing down upon him, was not really there. He thought as far as he could into the darkness between the clouds, and then as far again. There was no end to whatever it was he was looking into. As he watched, the sky opened a dark lid of cloud and looked down on him with a white lopsided, mad, moony eye. Pete and the night stared at one another, but the night looked away first – closing its clouds across the moon. Pete shut his own eyes quickly. Looking up suddenly from between the tombstones, he had taken infinity by surprise. Now, it made new, enormous, unending sense. He had seen the stars many times, but this time he felt they had altered him for ever.

Something rustled in the grass. It wasn't the wind. It was coming closer and closer . . . bony feet, perhaps, busily bustling towards him. Closer, . . . closer . . . right beside him! Pete screwed up his eyes, tighter and tighter, but then he felt he had to know the worst. His eyes sprang wide open as if his eyelids were on powerful springs. At the same moment he switched on the torch. Something small and spiky scuttled away from the light. A hedgehog!

There were no hedgehogs in Australia. This was the
first time in his life he had ever seen one.

Pete was so interested that he forgot his fear.
Sitting up, he tried to follow the hedgehog with
the torch. But it moved off quickly and, before he
could get a proper look at it, vanished into the night,
scrambling away on surprisingly long legs.

Seeing the hedgehog comforted Pete, though
he couldn't think why. It was like finding signs of
life on an unknown planet. Lying back again, he
thought spiky hedgehog thoughts rather than bony
graveyard ones, and perhaps he did go to sleep
accidentally. He couldn't quite remember, when he
thought about it afterwards. All he remembered was
that he was staring into the sky again. The clouds
had drifted by. The moon shone down.

The ground under the sleeping-bag seemed to
have grown lumpier and harder. He was warm
enough, but the earth's bones were coming up
through its skin of soil. Its ribs were grating against
his. Pete sat up and turned on the torch again.

Far away, on the other side of the hedge and the
Fortune family forest, he could hear voices singing.
His parents and grandparents, his uncles and aunts,
were singing old songs. Someone was playing a
banjo. That would be his father. Someone else was
playing a violin, and that must be Aunt Lorna. Pete

had often heard what a good fiddler she was.

'*I scream you scream, we all scream for ice cream,*' Pete heard them sing.

Out in the dark, Pete listened. He longed to be in the light with the singing and the laughter. After all, he was the one who knew all the words.

The bones of the earth pressed up through the sleeping-bag. Once more, Pete sat up and turned on the torch so that he could see how to work himself into a more comfortable position. He shone it on the stone on his right, and lit up the inscription on the headstone. Out of the corner of one eye, Pete made out sorrowful words: *sadly missed*. Above that, there was a name, partly in shadow, but still readable. Pete read it and froze. It was as if the stone were whispering to him.

Peter Tweed Fortune, aged ten. His own name! His own age! He was looking at his own gravestone. His travelling, family life, parents, Simon, Bombshell, and the cousins – they were nothing but dreams . . . the dreams of a ghost who mistakenly thought he was still alive. And at that moment, as he stared in horror, he heard footsteps . . . no, he *felt* footsteps. He felt them tremble in the ground, felt them running through his hands and into his arms and shoulders, then up his neck and into his head where they blundered like moths against a lighted window. No hedgehog, this time. Footsteps.

Pete turned his head away from the name on the tombstone and looked into the dark. A white blob was bouncing towards him, its edges fluttering in the graveyard wind.

CHAPTER ELEVEN

The white blob blobbed towards him. Pete fell flat on his back and lay there, wishing he were invisible. Little night breezes ran across his face.

Even if the ghost fell on him and he screamed, what good would it do? The Good Fortunes Gang would not come rushing to save him. The singing Fortunes would never hear him. A shriek rushed up through his throat, but he stopped it firmly with his teeth. Only a small, thin squeak got through to the outside world.

'Peter!' called an eerie voice. Nobody ever called him Peter. That was the name on the tomb.

Then another voice spoke.

'He'd never come here in a million years,' it said. 'Just living next door to the graveyard frightens him.'

That wasn't a ghost. That was Simon . . . Simon, whose blackness made him invisible in the night.

'Those *kids*!' exclaimed the first voice, sounding more ordinary this time. 'Oh, I think I've torn my lace tights!'

Peter felt the scream behind his teeth dissolve. He opened his mouth and all that came out was a little sigh. Then he sat up, and switched on the torch. Someone yelled with fright, but it wasn't him. It was Simon.

'Peter!' said the first voice, and this time it didn't sound strange. 'Wow! You nearly frightened the life out of us.' It was Prue. Beside her, Simon clasped his hands to his black chest as if he were struggling to keep his heart inside him. Prue looked cool and easy.

'Those pigs!' she cried. 'I could turn them all into bacon!'

'How did you know I was here?' asked Pete.

'Lolly heard the others talking earlier, and then she heard you going out. She didn't exactly want to tell tales on the others. But she crept out and came and told me so that I could get you back into bed before your mother came home and found you missing.'

'Just as well Mum didn't find your bed empty. She'd have been frantic,' said Simon. 'But I don't suppose you kids thought of that.'

'You have to go through the test to join the gang,' said Pete.

'No, you don't,' said Prue scornfully. 'None of them would ever spend a night in a graveyard, even a friendly one.'

'Friendly!' exclaimed Pete softly, looking around. 'A graveyard *friendly*?'

'Well, this one's friendly,' said Prue. 'There are a lot of Fortunes here! I used to play on their graves when I was little.'

'Anyhow, I'm the only one that's allowed to give you nightmares,' Simon said. 'That's a brother's job, not a cousin's.'

'That stone's got my name on it,' Pete said, pointing.

'Far out!' said Simon. Pete saw him shiver a little as he read the headstone.

'It's a great-uncle,' said Prue. 'Uncle Peter was named after that Peter, and you're named after Uncle Peter, so I suppose in a way it *is* your name. But it's not *you* that's buried there. That particular poor Peter drowned years ago. They found him in the sea, and brought him home. So he's here, right next door to the rest of us.'

She held out her hand to Pete.

'Come on! I'll take you round and introduce you, so you know this non-singing part of the family. It'll be another sort of family reunion.'

Pete crawled out of the sleeping-bag, feeling like a butterfly stepping out of a cocoon. Prue gathered up the sleeping-bag and handed it to Simon who tossed it over his shoulder.

'You take charge of the torch,' Prue told Pete. He and Simon followed her past little mossy fences, and headstones like scattered pages. Some of them were decorated with white stone flowers set under glass domes. Pete saw stone doves, and clasped hands, nestling among the flowers.

Prue stopped in front of a stone as big as a double bed.

'Great-Grandpa and Great-Grandma Fortune!' she cried. 'I used to dance on this stone when I was little.'

'Dance?' said Simon, a disapproving vampire.

'Well, if it were me I'd like to feel great-grandchildren close by,' Prue answered. 'I'd say, "Go on! Dance! Dance! Let my bones feel you dancing."'

By now the moon was shining down so brightly that Pete switched off the torch to save the battery. They moved on with Prue pointing out family names on headstones, like chapter headings in a rambling story.

'Of course, I've other relations here who aren't Fortunes,' she said over her shoulder. 'But tonight's Fortune night.'

There were graves of old Fortunes, and graves of young ones . . . even the graves of three babies that had not lived long enough to be given names. *Baby Fortune* it said on each of their headstones.

Prue sounded so fond of the stones and the buried relations that it suddenly seemed to Pete that he too had known them for a long, long while. Through the trees they could faintly hear Fortune family songs being sung in their grandparents' house.

'When Father papered the parlour, you couldn't
see Pa for paste.
Dabbing it here! Dabbing it there! Paste and paper
everywhere.
Mother got stuck to the ceiling, the kids got stuck
to the floor.

You never saw a blooming family so stuck up
    before!'
'They're singing the old songs,' said Prue.
'We know them,' said Simon proudly. 'Well, Pete
knows every one of them by heart.'
The song stopped suddenly but none of them
took any notice.
They had moved in a wide circle and were
standing by the gap in the hedge through which
Tracey, Jackson, Tessa and Pete had entered the
graveyard. The old fenced grave with the missing
picket was still grinning at them, but by now its grin
was a friendly one.
There was a loud bump on the other side of the
hedge.
Pete turned to Prue. Simon drew a deep breath.
Prue merely put her finger across her lips and
stepped back into the shadows.
'He'll be scared, scared, scared,' said a voice in a
whispered chant. 'I'll bet he's quaking. I'll bet he's
shaking.'
A figure with pale hair pushed itself through the
hedge. It was followed by another one, and then a
third, darker figure.
'Not too close,' Tracey said. 'We'll stand in the
shadows and moan.'
'Oh, man!' said Jackson. 'He'll be scared. Not

just a little bit scared, but *big* scared, *enormous* scared, *infinity* scared.'

He doesn't even know what infinity means, thought Pete in amazement, looking at Simon. But I do . . . I looked right at it and it looked back at me. It's gone now, but I know it's there.

Simon and Peter both looked at Prue. It seemed they could all understand each other without saying a word.

'He's going to be aghast,' Jackson went on as he and Tracey moved by so close to Pete that he could have touched them. 'A guest aghasted by a ghost. A guest a-ghosted by a ghost.'

He was dancing a little, but Pete knew – knew for certain – that Jackson was the ghast ready to be a-ghosted by the guest. He, Pete, was the guest who was going to a-ghost him.

'It's a bit mean,' said Tessa. 'I mean, he hasn't done anything to us.'

'He's taken my bedroom,' Tracey hissed. 'Ready? One! Two! Three!' she peered towards the place where she thought Pete was still lying. 'Moan!'

Slowly, Prue lifted her arm. Simon and Pete watched it rise through shadows shot with moonlight.

Tracey and Jackson began a weird moaning . . . a terrible sound that would have horrified Pete if

he had still been lying on his own between the two gravestones, being looked at by infinity.

Prue brought her arm down as if she were conducting an orchestra.

Simon cackled hideously, Pete howled. Together, all three of them leaped out of the darkness on to Tracey, Tessa and Jackson.

'Gotcha!' shouted Prue.

Three shrieks of terror rose up out of the old graveyard.

And at that moment, faintly but clearly, Pete heard someone far off in the darkness call his name.

CHAPTER TWELVE

Jackson fell in a heap on the ground and lay there mumbling, 'Man, oh man, oh man!' Even in his terror he twitched, as if he were dancing. Rather more slowly, Tessa collapsed beside him, both hands clasped across her face.

Tracey, panting, looked at Prue, Pete and Simon.

'So you scared me! Big deal!' She did her best to sound ordinary, but her voice was high and trembling.

'You were being unkind to a *cousin*,' said Prue, taking the torch from Pete and shining it straight into Tracey's face.

'We were just testing him,' said Tracey.

'Suppose his mother had found he was missing?' asked Prue. 'She'd have been worried frantic. And anyway, you kids shouldn't be wandering round in the dark.'

'Back before you were married, you used to sneak out and go to parties,' said Tracey rebelliously.

'Man, oh man! I'm dead!' sighed Jackson, still lying on the ground and writhing in time to his own words. 'Dead, dead and never been wed.'

'Dead, dead and out of bed!' Pete said so that other people could hear his rhymes, as well. In the torchlight he saw Jackson's eyes snap open. He stared up at Pete as if this new cousin had spoken a secret password.

'It's because I used to be so silly that I know it *is* silly to sneak out at night,' said Prue to Tracey. Tracey pulled a scornful face.

'Great!' she said. 'You've turned into a grown-up.'

'That's right,' Prue agreed. 'I *am* grown up. And you're just a kid. And you were being *cruel*.'

'Not cruel!' cried Tracey. But for the first time she sounded ashamed. 'It's just that he's a . . . well, he's only just come here and he's living in the old house, and sleeping in my old room that I didn't want to leave, *and* he's been having a party in his honour.'

Jackson scrambled to his feet.

'What a night!' he said. 'What a night, what a night! What a terrible fright.'

'My heart nearly stopped, but it didn't quite,' finished Pete. Jackson turned and stared at Pete once more. Then, slowly, he began to grin. Tracey took no notice of them. She wheeled round on Tessa.

'Did you tell on us?' she asked.

'*I* saw you kids setting off,' Prue replied, lying a little. 'Come on, Trace. You were being mean to a new cousin.'

'Pete!' called a faint, distant voice. Pete heard it distinctly. His ear was trained to hear his mother calling.

'Well, it's like that prodigal-son story,' Tracey complained. 'My dad stayed at home and helped the grandys, and he's never once had a party in his honour. It's not fair.'

'Being mean to a cousin doesn't make it any fairer,' said Prue severely.

'Come on, you kids! Where are you hiding?'

shouted another voice – a man's voice. It was far off – on the other side of the house, but this time Prue, Simon, Jackson, Tracey and Tessa heard it, too.

'Oh, spattzz!' said Pete and Simon together.

'They know we've gone!' cried Jackson.

'They were singing just a moment ago,' Tracey said, looking around as if uncles and aunts might suddenly appear out of the shadows.

'I expect your mothers came over to check up on you, and found you were gone,' said Prue. She turned away, cupped her hands over her mouth and shouted, 'Over here! They're over here.'

'Coo-ee!' called Pete.

'You sound Australian,' said Jackson, looking pleased.

Somewhere, someone heard them. They heard a voice call, 'Findlay, they're on the other side of the house.'

Tracey looked sideways at Pete. 'We're up the creek now,' she said scowling. 'My lot'll be really mad with me.'

'Me, too,' Pete said. 'But it was good to get out of bed and come down here. That's the sort of thing you can do at home, even at midnight.'

As he said it, he felt for the first time that he was at home. Tracey might have been trying to frighten him, but her test had worked in a way she hadn't expected. It had broken a spell. For one thing, Pete knew he would never be afraid of the graveyard again. It seemed to him that he could feel his past family lying peacefully in the land behind him as the present family came storming towards him through the night. There would never, ever be any bony fingers reaching through the hedge to try and grab him as he went past. The angels looking over the hedge were smiling because they were pleased to see him.

Tracey was watching him. Pete could tell she was trying to work out if he were mad at her and what he was going to tell the grown-ups. In the torchlight he could see the beginning of a smile, but not an angelic one. It was too mischievous for any angel – a little bit ashamed and a little bit shy.

She opened her mouth to say something, but then they all heard approaching voices. Footsteps thudded around the corner of the house. A stronger light swept across the house side of the hedge. Bits of it slipped through the leaves and fell in a scattered, jiggling jigsaw puzzle of brightness around them.

'I thought I heard someone screaming!' an aunt was saying.

'It was just us chickens cackling,' called Prue.

Turning, she struggled through the gap in the hedge. Tracey, Jackson, Tessa, Simon and Pete

followed her. On the other side of the hedge
the light seemed as bright as a small sun. Pete
couldn't see past it, but he recognized the voices.
He turned off his own torch. On the other side
of the hedge were his uncles, aunts, grandparents
and parents. For the last time that night he looked
over his shoulder and smiled at the dead Fortune
family, before climbing through to the live ones.

'It was just one of those midnight *worraworras!*'
Tracey was saying. 'Fortune kids always have a
worraworra!'

Worraworra worraworraworra was what Tigger had
said outside Pooh's house when he was a stranger
in the forest. *Worraworra* was what Fortune children
had cried to one another, playing hide-and-seek in
the darkened house. '*Worraworra!*' they would growl,
crawling from room to room, making a scary party
for themselves.

'We were crawling around in the dark trying to
find each other,' explained Pete, backing up Tracey,
and it suddenly seemed a brilliant description of what
had really been going on.

'And you did find each other, even out here?'
asked an uncle. Pete recognized Uncle Peter's voice.

'Well, I found a few people,' said Simon.

'Me, too,' said Trace the Ace, and she smiled
sideways, slyly, at Pete.

'Oh, Pete,' said his mother. 'Why do you frighten me like this? It was nearly as bad as the time you tied that rope from the chimney to the tree and tried to slide along it.'

'Did you try to slide from the *roof*?' asked Tracey.

'Don't growl at him, Maddy,' said Pete's father. 'It wouldn't have been a real family reunion without a *worraworra*.'

'Well, I'll forgive them this time,' said Maddy. 'And I'm going inside to make a cup of tea. This is a formal invitation for everyone to have one with me . . . if I can find a few cups, that is.'

There was a chorus of agreement from the other Fortunes, and they all began to drift towards the house that was now Pete's house.

'You're never, never to sneak out at night again,' he heard someone telling Tracey. Pete knew without turning around that it was Aunt Tiffany, and realized that he was beginning to know just who was who.

CHAPTER THIRTEEN

A little later, Pete sat in the shadows of the hall with all his cousins around him . . . except one, that is. Tracey seemed to have wandered off on her own.

Pete was sharing the bottom step of the stairs with Tessa. Lolly, who had been waiting for them when they all came trooping in, sat on the step above them. Pete's hands were clasped around a small enamel bowl of weak tea, enjoying its warmth.

None of the houses he had lived in had ever had such a big kitchen. The bottom step of the stairs was like a seat in a theatre, and the kitchen, its door wide open, was like a lighted stage. Fortunes sat around the big table in the middle of the room, or sometimes even on the table. Other Fortunes had settled themselves on packing cases, drinking tea from anything Maddy had been able to find. Maddy herself had her tea in a small jug, and Toby held a vase. There's something about drinking tea out of jugs and vases – because no-one can remember just which packing case the cups are in – that stops people being too cautious with one another. What was going on in the kitchen was even more of a family reunion than the gathering on the lawn next door. Sitting on the bottom step of the stairs, Pete listened carefully, disentangling what the Fortune family were saying to one another. Only one person seemed to be worried about the happenings of the evening.

'But listen,' Uncle Ivor was saying, 'they all went wandering around in the dark when they were supposed to be in bed. Suppose there had been some sort of accident?' He had been given tea in a small pottery bowl, and as he talked, he looked down at it with a puzzled frown as if he wasn't quite sure how it had got into his hands.

'Oh, Ivor, don't be so stuffy,' said Aunt Lorna. 'We Fortune kids often used to get out of bed and have a *worraworra* in the bush.'

'It's almost as if we had had a *worraworra* all over again ourselves,' Uncle Findlay was saying to Toby. 'Remember that time when . . . ?'

'It was just dreadful when I looked into his room and saw he was missing,' Maddy was telling Prue. 'I thought he had run away. Trying to get back to Brisbane, perhaps.'

'Brisbane! When he's got the chance of living in Fairfield?' said Prue laughing. 'No way! He'll never want to go back there again.'

'Are you kidding?' said Maddy. 'Queensland's full of New Zealanders trying to get away from the cold.'

'I was sure they'd be in the bush somewhere,' Grandma Fortune was saying to Aunt Marama. 'I never once thought of the graveyard.'

'I knew it would be something to do with

Tracey,' Aunt Tiffany exclaimed, interrupting
Maddy and Prue. She was holding her baby, Angel,
in her arms. Maddy was holding Bombshell, and
Prue was holding Janey. The three babies, all girls,
looked solemnly at one another.

In the doorway, half in, half out of the kitchen,
leaned Simon. Pete felt sorry for him. There were
no cousins of his own age to talk to, and he no
longer had the fun of teasing Pete about ghosts and
graveyards. Pete helped himself to a finger of toast
and a sliver of cheese from the plate at his feet. At
least his mother had found the toaster. He noticed
Tessa frowning down at his plate.

'We'll get biscuits later on today,' he said.

'I like toast,' said Tessa. 'I was just looking for the
best piece.'

Jackson, who was sitting on the step behind them,
leaned over and breathed toastcrumbs into Pete's ear.

'Man, you scared the life out of me,' Jackson said.
'My heart just stopped. Bang! Then it started off
again, rapping away twice as fast. Wicked, man, just
wicked!'

'But you were trying to scare *him*,' said Lolly. 'It's
fair that he scared you back.'

'Oh, yeah! I know,' said Jackson. 'But man, oh
man! You let that scream off in my ear, and wow!
Bang! I nearly died of fright.'

'One moment frightened of a ghost, and now you're eating buttered toast,' said Pete.

'Right on, man!' cried Jackson, laughing heartily.

Pete thought his mother looked much happier and easier than she had earlier that day. As for his father, he and Uncle Findlay and Uncle Peter were loudly criticizing one another.

'That's just like you!' 'What absolute rubbish!' 'How can you tell? *You've* never even been out of New Zealand.' 'Well, all I can say is, Australia's rotted your brain, mate.' Their voices rose and fell, but they were laughing. They sounded much more like brothers than they had on the lawn next door.

Jackson lurched sideways. Someone had come downstairs, pushing past him as if he were merely a branch in the way.

'It's funny,' said Tracey's voice over Pete's head. 'I've just been looking into my old room, but it doesn't feel like mine any more. Without our things it doesn't look like home.' She bent over the plate of toast and took two pieces. As she did this she looked sideways at Pete and pulled an unexpectedly funny face. Pete could barely see her in the shadows, but he knew it was a sign of goodwill.

His old nightmare and the horror of all the familiar things deserting him flitted into his head, but it had no power to frighten him now. Tracey,

Jackson and Tessa hadn't actually said that they would let him join the Good Fortunes Gang, but he could feel that he was one of them now. He was a Fortune, sitting in the light of the kitchen with a family around him.

Suddenly, the idea of having a big family took hold of him, and with the idea came an unexpected plan. Tomorrow he would begin making a family tree, and nobody would be left off. He would mark in his Australian relations, too, and all the people who had names other than Fortune. And when he was properly settled in as a member of the Good Fortunes Gang, he would make them allow Lolly to be a gang member, too. He'd have to wait for a while, of course. He knew it was a mistake to throw one's weight around too soon. Still, he would do it.

As for the false sister, she would never be a menace or a mystery again. She was just his cousin, Tracey. And though she had tried to frighten him, he had actually frightened her. He had turned her own trick back on her. From now on, this house would hold the family who lived in it safe during the hours of darkness. And the town would hold the house, and the stars and the sea would hold the town, and the universe would hold the stars and the sea. No-one could be much more secure than that . . . being held by the universe. And everyone would be able to sleep peacefully.

Sitting there among his cousins, Pete knew that he had come home at last, while outside in the moonlight on the quiet hillside, other Fortunes – old people and children, and some in between – slept peacefully, too, still remembered, still part of the family, and still safe at home.